Impressions of School
がっこうのうた

日航財団＝編
Edited by The JAL Foundation

ブロンズ新社
Bronze Publishing

『地球は学校なのだ』

日本学生俳句協会　代表　水野 あきら

はじめに

ハワイから寄せられた句にこんなのがある。

School is like magic
Entering worlds of knowledge
Finding our dreams now

と、ずばり「学校」とはそうなんだよと、テーマを直接法で結びつけて表現している。この"school"はすなわち"teacher"でもある。

この子が用いた"magic"がどの程度の深度で詠み込まれた用語であるのかうかがい知れないが、この句をタネに、ある年配者の集会で提起してみた。「学校」から連想する情景や感触は？」との問いに、出るわ出るわ。先生・校長・試験・参観日・みちくさ・宿題・遅刻・遠足・運動会・通信簿・保健室・初恋……等々と、そのとどまるところを知らない。それらの一語一語に、喜びも悲しみも投影されているだろうことを思う時、学校とは、喜怒哀楽を盛り込む器だなと実感する。だから先生とは、心情の映りの濃度を仕分ける分析試薬のようなものだなと、自身の来し方を思い浮かべながら、改めて思いを深くした。

そういえば、次のような句がある。

小小泥娃娃
没有爸爸没有妈
我来抚养他

詠者が十歳のころの句で、今ではきっと大活躍の青年のはずである。この表現に潜む「愛」とその「眼差し」

は、汚れのない子ども時代だからこそ発せられた優しさと正義感だと、私は素直に感動する。『このドロ人形には父ちゃんも母ちゃんもいない。だったら私が育ててあげる！』の心根が嬉しい。人間、長ずるに従って忘れていく「愛」の原点を、花に虫に、そしてドロ人形にだって注ごうとした「子ども心」に還元させて、質の本源をたどろうとする時、そこに「詩」が生まれると信じて疑わない。古今のすぐれた詩人たちが、そして日本の俳人たちが口をそろえて「子ども心」の本流の尊さを訴えている。そういえば、科学者も言う。「子どもの『なぜ』が科学研究の本源である」と。

一九九〇年刊行の『地球歳時記』の結びでは次のように述べられている。

「二十一世紀を担うこども達がそれぞれの土地で自然と心の交流の所産として……ハイクを通して……豊かな平和な社会を願う地球人に育っていくこと……『地球環境』および『自然生命』が二十一世紀最大の重要な課題となる……ハイクはその課題を認識するにもまったくふさわしい詩型……」と。当時、俳壇の動きの中にもまったくなかった「地球歳時記」構想は、日航財団の編み出した世界視野にたつ平和建設塔であったと、敬してここに紹介し、本書に刻まれた子どもたちのハイクが、どうか平和の使徒となってくれることを期待し祈りたい。

そうなのだ、地球は学校だったのだ！

Prologue

"The Earth is a School"

Akira Mizuno Director of Japanese Students Haiku Association

The poet expresses what "school" is all about by directly linking the theme and his image. "School" in this sense is the same thing as "teacher." I have no idea as to the depth of the poet's thoughts behind the word 'magic' in this haiku, but I was inspired to ask a group of elderly people to share with me what they think of when they hear the word 'school'. The group produced an endless stream of responses: teacher, principal, tests, parents' day, playing with friends on the way home, homework, being late for school, field trip, sports day, report card, infirmary, first love, etc. When I think about how all the joys and sorrows of school days are reflected in each of these expressions, I realize that school is a receptacle where a vast array of emotions is brought into. Looking back on my own experience as a teacher, I come to think again that a teacher is something like a chemical agent that reveals the strength and nature of the students' sentiments.

This reminds me of another haiku that was originally composed in Chinese:

This mud doll
Has no dad or mom
So I'll raise it

It was made by a 10-years-old, who must be a successful young adult by now. I was impressed, and continue to be impressed, by the 'love' and 'insight' embodied in this haiku, which I believe is a gentleness and sense of justice stemming only from the innocence of childhood. This heart – this desire to want to bring up a parentless mud doll - makes me happy. As we grow older, we tend to lose touch with the source of love.

When we attempt to re-capture the heart of a child, the spirit of love which a child often pours to flowers, insects and even to a mud doll, I have no doubt that this is the moment when a poem is born. Eminent poets of all ages, including Japanese haiku poets, have all spoken of the value of the innocence of childhood. Scientists also know that the source of scientific research lies in the inquisitive mind of the child – the mind that seeks the "why and the wherefore."

In the closing remark of the JAL Foundation's "Haiku by World Children '90", its first volume, we can see words such as:

"...inspiring children, who are the actual builders of the 21st century, to create haiku as an end result of correspondence between men and nature ....and fostering children through haiku to become global people committed to an affluent and peaceful society. ... 'earth environment' and 'life in nature' becoming the most important problem of the 21st century.... haiku has the possibility of becoming the most universal of poetry form to highlight these crucial problems..."

Back in 1990, there was no idea of World Children's Haiku in the haiku circles of Japan. I am proud to present it as a peace-building monument with a global scope, thoughtfully initiated by Japan Airlines. I hope and pray that these haiku by world children introduced in this volume will become apostles of world peace.

Yes, that's right. The earth is indeed a school.

1章 がっこうがはじまるよ
School starts

学校はお母さんみたい
みんなを愛して教えてくれる
うれしくて駆(か)けていく

The school is like mother
Loves and teaches everyone
I run to her with joy

Школа, как мама,
Всех любит и учит.
Бегу к ней с радостью

●●●●●

Scherbakova Dasha
age9　Female　Russia（ロシア）

国名は居住国を示します。Country name indicates the place of residence.

春風と
手をつなぎゆく
ランドセル

School rucksacks
And spring breeze
Going home hand in hand
・・・・・

津波古　陽介
Yousuke Tsuhako
age13　Male
Japan（日本）

いちめんの花
学校にそよ風ふいて
冬にさよなら

Blossoms are everywhere
Fresh breeze even in the school
Good-bye wintertime

Blüten überall
frischer Wind selbst in der Schul'
Winterzeit ade

・・・・・

Caroline Weinz
age13　Female
Germany（ドイツ）

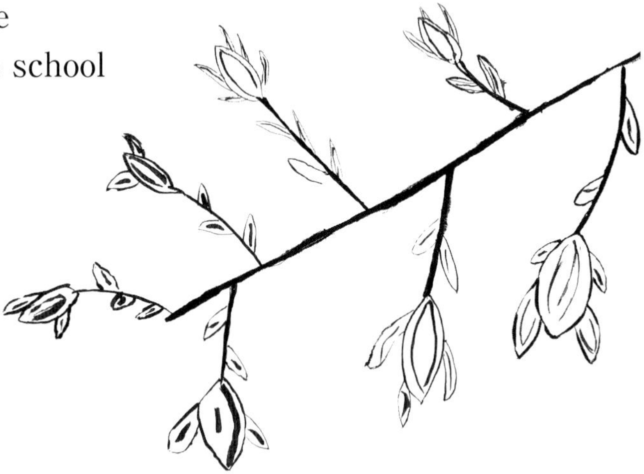

みあげると
さくらのはっぱが
だんすする

Looking up cherry trees
Leaves are dancing
In a gentle breeze

・・・・・

藤井　妙江
Tae Fujii
age4　Female　Japan（日本）

The peach blossoms in spring
Laughters fulfill the school every corner
You & I celebrate the joy

春天桃花開
校園歡笑處處在
你我同慶賀

Yuen Ching Ho
age9　Female
China（中国）

春にさく桃の花
学校中に笑いがあふれ
あなたと私も喜び祝う

かたつむりさん
学校にちこくした
24時間おくれてる

The snails are little bit late
To the school
For twenty-four hours

Улитки в школу
Чуть-чуть опаздывают:
На сутки.

● ● ● ● ●

Besedina Sasha
age6　Female
Russia(ロシア)

On my first long day
I cried and cried all day long
Till it was home time
· · · · ·
Cullum Myles
age9　Male
England（イギリス）

学校の
初日(しょにち)は泣いてた
かえるまで

On first day of new semester
Dad entered pawnshop
While I broke open my piggy bank

โรงเรียนเปิดวันแรก
พ่อเดินเข้าโรงรับจำนำ
หมูน้อยฉันถูกทุบ

・・・・・

Thanakrit Muangsri
age11　Male
Thailand（タイ）

新学期
ブタの貯金箱あけるぼく
質屋へ向かうお父さん

My heart is pumping
My hands are sweaty
It is the first day fo school

・・・・・

Bella Huggins
age11　Female
Australia（オーストラリア）

胸ドキドキ
両手汗ばむ
始業の日

Summer holidays ending
Please extend
Just another day

・・・・・

木立　椋
Ryo Kidachi
age 10　Male
Japan（日本）

夏休み
後一日だけ
えん長を

地震(じしん)が学校をゆらす
めちゃくちゃにされても
読書への愛はこわれない

Earthquakes shook the school
But not our love to read books
School on the ruines

・・・・・
Rachel Ying
age14　Female
USA（アメリカ）

あふれる知性
夢かなう
未来は思うがまま

Flowing Intelligence
Fullfillment of all my dreams
Tomorrow everywhere

Daluyan dunong
Pangarap katuparan
Bukas saanman

・・・・・

Maria Frencheska Nueva
age12　Female
Philippines（フィリピン）

Small steps before entering school
Gain knowledge from teachers
Bigger steps in the future

ก้าวเล็กก่อนเข้าเรียน
รับความรู้จากครูที่สอน
สู่ก้าวที่ยิ่งใหญ่

· · · · ·

Sireejitt Srisuwan
age11　Female
Thailand（タイ）

入学前の小さな一歩
先生からたくさん教わって
やがて大きなステップに

鎌（かま）を手にした父さん母さん
稲穂（いなほ）かきわけ
田んぼのなかの学校へ

Scythes in hand Mom and Dad lead
Through the field of rice ears
To our school in the rice fields

ลมพัดรวงข้าวไหว
แม่พ่อถือเคียวเดินนำหน้า
โรงเรียนกลางทุ่งนา

● ● ● ● ●

Mata Jakpeng
age11　Female　Thailand（タイ）

花がわたしをのぞきこむ
勉強してるのに
花に心をうばわれる

The flower looks at me
She is planted in my dreams
When I study

La fleur me regarde
Elle est plantée dans mes rêves
Quand je travaille

● ● ● ● ●

Alessandra Landogna
age9　Female
Morocco（モロッコ）

The smell of rose
Floating our school garden
Melted my sorrow

•••••

Keymon Robinson
age10　Male
USA（アメリカ）

バラの香り
校庭をつつみ
かなしみ癒す

秋、冬、春……
毎年つづく
十一年間の学校時代

Autumn, winter, spring...
Year after year
Eleven school years

Осень, зима, весна…
Так одиннадцать лет –
Школьные годы.

▪ ▪ ▪ ▪ ▪

Zaitseva Natalya
age13　Female
Russia（ロシア）

2日間泊まってた
エコ・ガーデンの蛾が
今日でさようなら

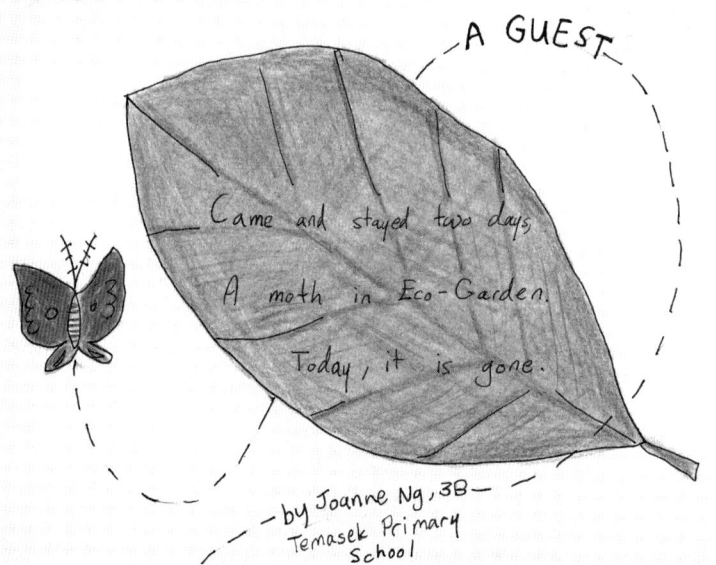

Came and stayed two days
A moth in Eco-Garden
Today, it is gone

・・・・・

Joanne Ng
age8　Female
Singapore（シンガポール）

The little beast
Stuck the nose out of the hole
It's time to learn life

Малыш-зверек
Высунул нос из норки –
Пора учиться жить.

・・・・・

Nikitin Fyodor
age8　Male　Russia（ロシア）

穴から鼻を出した
ちいさな動物
生きるための勉強をしなくちゃ

ヒューヒューと冬の風
生徒を学校へと追いたてる
大声で高く低く朗読しながら

The winter wind whistled
Urging the students to go to school
Reading aloud high and low

北風呼呼吹
催促學子進學堂
書聲響朗朗

●●●●●

Agape Luk
age10　Female　China（中国）

Run, run as the wind
Wiping the sweat from my face
Never late for school

● ● ● ● ●

Martin Lee
age8　Male　China（中国）

風のように走れ
ひたいの汗をぬぐって
ぜったい学校におくれるな

学校へと向かう道
雪が顔に吹きつける
始(し)業(ぎょう)ベルがなっている

I walk down the road
The snow blows against my face
I hear the school bell

・・・・・

Miles Dover
age12　Male
New Zealand（ニュージーランド）

小さな木から葉が落ちる
戦争は学校をなくし
生きる術(すべ)もうばいとる

Leaves fall from small trees
Sad war means no school for some
No skills to lead life
・・・・・

Gill Ramneet
age13　Female　England（イギリス）

炸裂する爆弾音
校舎の下のシェルターに急ぐ
先生の無事を祈りながら

Bomb threatening explosions sound
Rush me to shelter under school building
Wish our teachers safety

เสียงระเบิดตูมตาม
วิ่งหลบอยู่ใต้อาคารเรียน
อย่าทำร้ายครูฉัน

· · · · ·

Kaennita Kambud
age11　Female　Thailand（タイ）

Do I have my lunch
Do I have my homework done
Traffic jam I'm late

・・・・・

Harry White
age12　Male
New Zealand（ニュージーランド）

お弁当持った
宿題も終わってる
でも渋滞でぼく遅刻

Piled up lilke a mountain
Homework load reaches its height
I am buried

・・・・・

Yi Kai Choo
age10　Male
Singapore（シンガポール）

宿題の山
最高峰に達し
ぼく埋まる

昼休みのベル、食堂へいそぐ
スープがこぼれて
かかっちゃった

Recess bell has rung
Run to the canteen for food
Spills soup over me

● ● ● ● ●

Darren Yeo
age6　Male
Singapore（シンガポール）

屋根は空
環境(かんきょう)は先生
地球という名のぼくらの学校

Our roof is the sky
Environment is our teacher
Our school is named Earth

ท้องฟ้าเป็นหลังคา
สิ่งที่อยู่รอบตัวเป็นครู
โรงเรียนนี้ชื่อโลก

• • • • •

Komkrid Saekong
age11　Male　Thailand（タイ）

日が暮れて
世界のお話をきく
おばあちゃんのひざ枕で

At night fall I rest my head
On Grandma's lap enjoying her tales
Stories about universal wonders

ค่ำลงหนุนตักยาย
ฟังเรื่องเล่านิทานดวงดาว
จากโรงเรียนท้องฟ้า

● ● ● ● ●

Dararat Khamjing
age11　Female
Thailand（タイ）

一歩ずつ
ワクワクドキドキ
始業(しぎょう)の日

Step by step I walk
Excited and nervous, on
The first day of school

● ● ● ● ●

Gwynette Paez
age12　Female
USA（アメリカ）

School

Step by step I walk
Excited and nervous, on
The first day of school

学校へ行く
空は晴天
でも学校へ行く

I go to school
The weather is fine
But I go to school

Я иду в школу.
Погода хорошая,
Но иду в школу.

• • • • •

Kuzmin Fedya
age10　Male
Russia（ロシア）

七時だよ！
はやく起きなきゃ！
学校がはじまるよ

Come on it's seven o'clock!
Hurry and get up!
It's time for school

Su son le sette!
Sbrigati ad alzarti!
E′ ora di scuola

• • • • •

Valeria Fusco
age11　Male
Italy（イタリア）

学校大好き
土日なんてなくていいのに
いつもそう思ってる

My strong attachment to my school
I wish there was no Saturday or Sunday
That's what I always long for

โรงเรียนในดวงใจ
ไม่อยากให้มีเสาร์อาทิตย์
หลับก็ยังฝันถึง

• • • • •

Patcharaporn Bootrod
age11　Female
Thailand（タイ）

おじいちゃんもおとうさんも
学校に通った
だからぼくも通うよ

My grandfather attended school
My father attended school
I attend school

Дедушка ходил в школу,
Папа ходил в школу,
Я хожу в школу…

• • • • •

Samsonov Kostya
age7　Male
Russia（ロシア）

仏教校の生徒たち
旗(はた)の下でお経を唱えてる
ああ、私はイスラム教徒

At Buddhist-oriented schools
Students chant a prayer at the flagpole
Alas, I am a Muslim

โรงเรียนวิถีพุทธ
นักเรียนสวดมนตร์หน้าเสาธง
ฉันเป็นมุสลิม

● ● ● ● ●

Pattamon Pattanaitsaraporn
age11　Female
Thailand（タイ）

学校は私の木
空高くまでのぼり
星をつかまえる

The school is my tree
To climb up to the high sky
And pick up the stars

● ● ● ● ●

Selin Mihaloglu
age11　Turkey（トルコ）

学校は
百合(ゆり)の芽(め)育てる
母のよう

School is like a second mother
Who makes us educated and united
Just like a new-born spout of lilly

La scuola è come la seconda mamma,
che ci cresce istruiti e uniti proprio
come un germoglio di giglio appena nato

● ● ● ● ●

Leda Orengo
age10　Female　Italy（イタリア）

知識の海
みんなのよろい
ぼくの学校

My school
A sea of intelligence
Weapon of John

Eskuwelahan
Dagat ng karunungan
Sandata ni Juan

・・・・・

Danielle Royon
age15　Male
Philippines（フィリピン）

ひとりひとり
ちがっていても
学校ではだれもが友だち

We are all different
But nobody is stranger
The school teachers to be friends

Мы разные,
Но нет среди нас чужих:
Школа учит дружить.

・・・・・

Rzhevkina Nina
age9　Female
Russia（ロシア）

ほうかごの
校ていとんぼが
ひとりじめ

After school
Dragonflies are monopolizing
Schoolyard

・・・・・

品川　瑞華
Mizuka Shinagawa
age8　Female
Japan（日本）

The first school picture
Two familiar white bows
Is it really me?

Первое школьное фото.
Два знакомых белых банта.
Неужели это я?

● ● ● ● ●

Muhametzyanova Elina
age14　Female
Russia（ロシア）

入学写真
見なれた白いちょうむすび
これ本当に私なの？

It's snowing slowly
And we are in a hurry to school
Textbooks and pens are waiting for us!

Снег падает медленно,
А мы торопимся в школу.
Учебники и ручки уже ждут нас!

● ● ● ● ●

Mescheryakova Agrippina
age9　Female
Russia（ロシア）

ゆっくりとふる雪
私たちは学校へいそぐ
教科書やペンがまっている！

The school bell cries out
But as distant memories
My friends are waiting

● ● ● ● ●

Morgan Adams
age12　Male
New Zealand（ニュージーランド）

始業(しぎょう)のベルがひびく
はるか昔の記憶(きおく)のなか
友人たちが待っている

Last leaf winter calls
School gates still open my mind
How I remember

● ● ● ● ●

Amelia Anderson
age13　Female
New Zealand（ニュージーランド）

冬を呼(よ)ぶ最後の落ち葉
今も校門を思い出す
どれほど覚えていることか

2章 クラスのなかでは
In the class room

むずかしい計算問題
やしの木みつめて
どうしよう？

I have a complicated calculation
I see a palm
What do I do ?

J'ai un calcul compliqué
Je regarde un palmier
Que faire ?

Charles Posez
age9　Male　Morocco（モロッコ）

ぴちゃぴちゃザーザー
うるさい雨のコンサート
勉強の気を散らす

Splash, splash, spash, trip, trip
The noisy rain concert
Distracts from learning

Platsch, platsch, platsch, bum, bum
Das laute Regenkonzert
lenkt vom Lernen ab

• • • • •

Jakob Schornholz
age11　Male
Germany（ドイツ）

冷たい空気
教室ではコート
冬が降りてきた

Bracing air
Coats in class
Winter has descended

L'aria frizzante
Cappotti in classe
Sceso l'inverno

• • • • •

Francesco Maria Picchi
age11　Male
Italy（イタリア）

外は雨
クラスみんなの音読(おんどく)の声で
鳥も虫もさえずる

Rain drizzling outside the windows
Surrounded by students reading sound
Birds and insects chirp

春雨窗外灑
同學朗讀聲片片
蟲鳥吱吱鳴

● ● ● ● ●

Po Nam Anson Lam
age10 Male
China（中国）

授業中
考えて絵を描く
わたしの創(そう)造(ぞう)力(りょく)

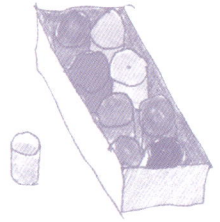

I have a lesson
I think and draw
My creativity

Я на уроке,
Думаю и рисую -
Моё творчество.

● ● ● ● ●

Danilova Ekaterina
age9　Female　Russia（ロシア）

40

子どもたちの笑い声
チャイムの音みたい
学校の休み時間

Children's laughter
Is like the ringing of bells
School break

Детский смех
Как колокольчиков звон.
Школьная перемена.

Baiguzina Yulia
age9　Female　Russia（ロシア）

Singing high and low
Fingers press black and white keys
Music class is fun

• • • • •

Tyler Caro
age6 Female
USA (アメリカ)

歌声に
けんばんおどる
音楽室

音楽の授業中
友だちが歌いはじめたら
窓辺(まどべ)の花がしおれちゃった

The lesson of music was going on
When my friend decided to sing a song
The flowers at the window have faded

Шёл урок музыки.
Мой друг решил запеть.
На окне завяли цветы.

· · · · ·

Surikov Oleg
age9　Male
Russia（ロシア）

音楽は
自分の内から
わきでる何か

The music is
Something that comes
From inside of you

La musica e'
Una cosa che viene
Da dentro di te

· · · · ·

Ilaria Paglia
age11　Female
Italy（イタリア）

鉛色(なまりいろ)の空から
ひとひらの雪
計算とけた

Just one flake of snow
Falls from the ice leaden sky
And maths turns to slush

• • • • •

Duggleby William
age12 Male
England（イギリス）

黒板いっぱいの文字
私をじろじろ
夢の中までおいかけてくる

Board is full of words
Words are all staring at me
Chasing in my dream

● ● ● ● ●

Wai Yann Lam
age10　Female
Singapore（シンガポール）

学校は
勉強だけじゃない
友情も生まれる

School is more than just
Learning how to read and write
Friendships are formed there

・・・・・

Georgina Sarah
age11　Female
Australia（オーストラリア）

学校では
友だちを愛することを教えるけど
大人たちはケンカばかり

The school cultivates children
To love and be friends to each other
Yet grown-ups tend to quarrel

โรงเรียนบ่มนิสัย
สอนให้รู้รักสามัคคี
ผู้ใหญ่ทะเลาะกัน

● ● ● ● ●

Phattaraporn Udjai
age11　Female　Thailand（タイ）

いたずらっ子のぼく
叱（しか）られてばかりだけど
先生が大好き

Stubbornness and naughtiness
Put me under frequent punishment
Yet I love my teacher

ผมดื้อและซุกซน
ครูตีกันบ่นเอือมระอา
แต่ผมก็รักครู

Napat Saeong
age11　Male　Thailand（タイ）

She is five years old
With bright blue bows in her hair
Mommy says goodbye

・・・・・

Hannah Hyunju Ban
age14　Female
New Zealand（ニュージーランド）

彼女は五才
髪に明るいブルーのリボン
バイバイってママがいう

Everything
Is many-coloured
But where is school uniform?

Какое все
Разноцветное...
Где же школьная форма.

・・・・・

Golubeva Alisa
age13　Female　Russia（ロシア）

色とりどりの
洋服を着たみんな
制服はどこへいった？

Форма школьника

机の上の本
文字がおどる
私の目はそれを見つめている

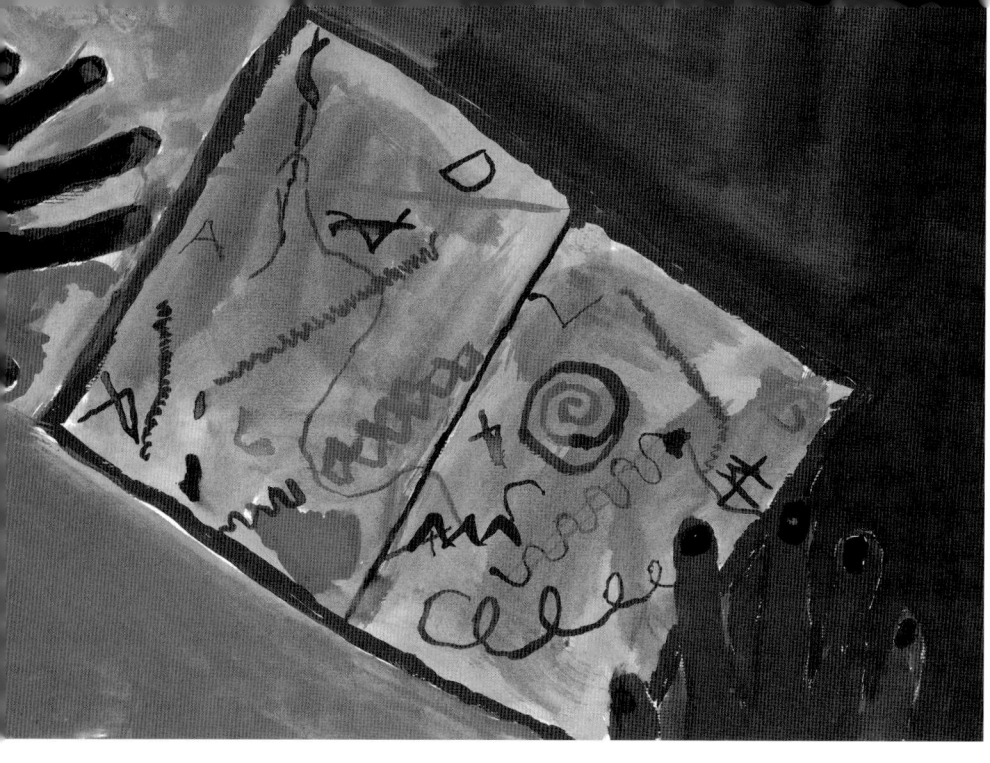

Books on the desk
The letters are dancing
The eye is watching them

Na mizi knjige
Črke imajo svoj ples
Oko jih gleda

• • • • •

Ferjančič Polona
age13　Female　Slovenia（スロベニア）

生徒たちは勉強中
えんぴつのたてる音
新しいことを学んでいる

Students are working
With the sound of pens writing
I learn something new

• • • • •

Kaitlin Jakson-Crates
age14　Female
New Zealand（ニュージーランド）

ぼくのつうしんぼで
ママ大爆発
居のこり勉強がまっている

With my report slip
Mum exploded into ash
Detention coming

・・・・・

Xu Ruo Gillian Chen
age10　Female
Singapore（シンガポール）

Exams drive me nuts!
Difficult sums here and there
But...do not give up!

・・・・・

Nadia Natasha Binte Abdul Rashid
age11　Female
Singapore（シンガポール）

テストでおかしくなりそう！
あっちもこっちも難問だらけ
でも……あきらめないぞ！

Daily I wait
Tensly for the loud gong
To end the lesson

Täglich warte ich
gespannt auf den lauten Gong
der die Stunde schließt

• • • • •

Michell Koczirka
age15　Male　Germany（ドイツ）

待ち遠しい
授業が終わる
鐘(かね)の音

The pen-stained whiteboard
Sitting in the dark corner
Longs to be dusted

● ● ● ● ●

Lester Michael
age13　Male
England（イギリス）

汚れたホワイトボードが
すみっこで
拭いてほしいとまっている

Paper plane is flying
It's a warm word
At lesson time

Самолётик летит.
Весточка теплая
Посреди урока.

● ● ● ● ●

Groza Lyuba
age14　Female
Russia（ロシア）

授業中に紙ひこうき
友だちからの
やさしいことば

Knowledge fills your mind
But so does breaktime gossip
Social life at stake

● ● ● ● ●

Woolf Ellen
age14　Female
England（イギリス）

うわさ話
楽しいけれど
仲間われ

Chills go down my back
Beads of sweat on my forehead
Report cards are here

● ● ● ● ●

Kerrick Chinen
age12　Male
USA（アメリカ）

背中ゾクッ
ひたいに冷や汗
つうしんぼ

School is safe the say
Uh Oh! Here come the bullies
I think I should hide!

・・・・・

Mia Smith
age11　Female
Australia（オーストラリア）

学校は安全というけれど
あっ！　いじめっ子
かくれなきゃ！

Please, teach me
The language of the stars
Old textbook

Научи меня
Языку звезд на небе,
Старый учебник.

● ● ● ● ●

Mohova Ekaterina
age15　Female
Russia（ロシア）

古い教科書さん
星たちのことばを
どうか教えて

I don't understand
Vast knowledge I gave away
But where's my reward

Bakit ba ganyan
Bayad ko'y kaalaman
Sukli'y nasaan

● ● ● ● ●

Princess Vhe Bacolod
age11　Female
Philippines（フィリピン）

たくさんの
知識(しき)をあげても
ごほうびなし

勉強が最優先(さいゆうせん)
学んで刺激(しげき)を受けるから
スポーツの試合(しあい)はヘトヘト

Work, tasks are prior
Live to learn and inspire
Sport games that tire

● ● ● ● ●

Victoria Lynn Chin
age 12　Female
Singapore（シンガポール）

Sometimes all my thoughts
Keep wandering from the school
To beloved blue sea

• • • • •

Anita Bagarić
age10　Female
Croatia（クロアチア）

教室から
思いはめぐる
青い海へ

No judgments
Getting out of scheme
Go ahead fantasy

Niente giudizi
Uscire dagli schemi
Vai, fantasia!

• • • • •

Caterina Cestari
age11　Male
Italy（イタリア）

まよわないで
とらわれないで
想像力を働かせよう！

The first day of school
The classrooms are humming with
Summer's memories

• • • • •

Lucia Pulek
age10　Female
Croatia（クロアチア）

新学期
みんなにぎやか
夏の思い出

Boats on moorings
Birds in the sky
Out the school window

• • • • •

Anderson Ivan
age7　Male
England（イギリス）

教室の
窓ごしに見る
船と鳥

Ring ring goes the bell
Rushing to the field squelching
In mud back to class

• • • • •

Hammond Amy
age14　Female
England（イギリス）

鐘(かね)がなり
泥(どろ)をはねはね
教室へ

ふりつもる雪で
学校は真っ白
喜びがこみあげる

The snow falls silenthly
The school is white
Joy fills us all

• • • • •

Cameron Smith
age12　Male
New Zealand（ニュージーランド）

During the endless rains
A rose sprouts out of the fence
Here comes the reading sound

春雨綿綿時
一枝薔薇出牆來
傳來讀書聲

・・・・・

Wai Ping Patricia Wong
age9　Female
China（中国）

ふりしきる雨
フェンスからバラが芽ぶく
朗読の声がきこえる

Butterfly closes to me
The bell of the school
Moves lightly

Un papillon près de moi
La cloche de l'école
Bouge légèrement

・・・・・

Linda Benkhelifat
age13　Male
France（フランス）

かたわらにちょうちょ
学校の鐘が
かろやかにゆれる

Hearing the clock tick
Watching trees bloom with flowers
Smelling today's lunch

・・・・・

Puniwaiwai Lua-Medeiros
age11　Female
USA（アメリカ）

時計の音をききながら
木に咲く花を見ながら
ランチのにおいをかいでいる

School is in the morning
Eating lunch is the best part
Then I eat at home

・・・・・

Cameron Flannery
age13　Male
New Zealand（ニュージーランド）

学校は午前中
最高なのはお昼の時間
家で食べられる

白いしっぽの猫が
校舎の窓の下にすわってる
先生になりたいのかな

A cat with a white tail
Is sitting under the school window
Wants to become a professor

Под школьным окном
Сидит кошка с белым хвостом.
Хочет стать учёной.

・・・・・

Konzhets Nikolai
age10　Male
Russia（ロシア）

ひとつぶの
なみだでめくる
次の章

A crystal tear
Turns the fragile pages
A new chapter starts

・・・・・

Stephanie Wong
age12　Female
Australia（オーストラリア）

木の椅子と
白いチョークに緑の黒板
それからＡＢＣＤ

There's a wooden chair
White Chalk and a green blackboard
And A B C D

May silyang kahoy
Yeso't berdeng pisara
At abakada

・・・・・

Patrick Sotto
age12　Male
Philippines（フィリピン）

教育の
香りさわやか
わが母校

School air refreshes
Smells like an education
School, part of my heart

・・・・・

Ethan Siegfried
age11　Male
USA（アメリカ）

3章 みんながそろえば
Eeverybody gets together

氷上のツリーハウス
冬休み中
雪合戦

Ice on the tree house
Many snowballs fly
White school break

Eis auf dem Baumhaus
viele Schneebälle sausen
weiße Schulpause

Lukas Maidhof
age11　Male　Germany（ドイツ）

School field day
I carry a relay baton
Heavy with our wishes to win

・・・・・

菅原　大嵩
Hirotaka Sugawara
age12　Male
Japan（日本）

運動会
思いをのせた
バトン持つ

Summer school camp
Taking off socks
Black and white feet

夏合宿
くつ下脱げば
黒と白

・・・・・

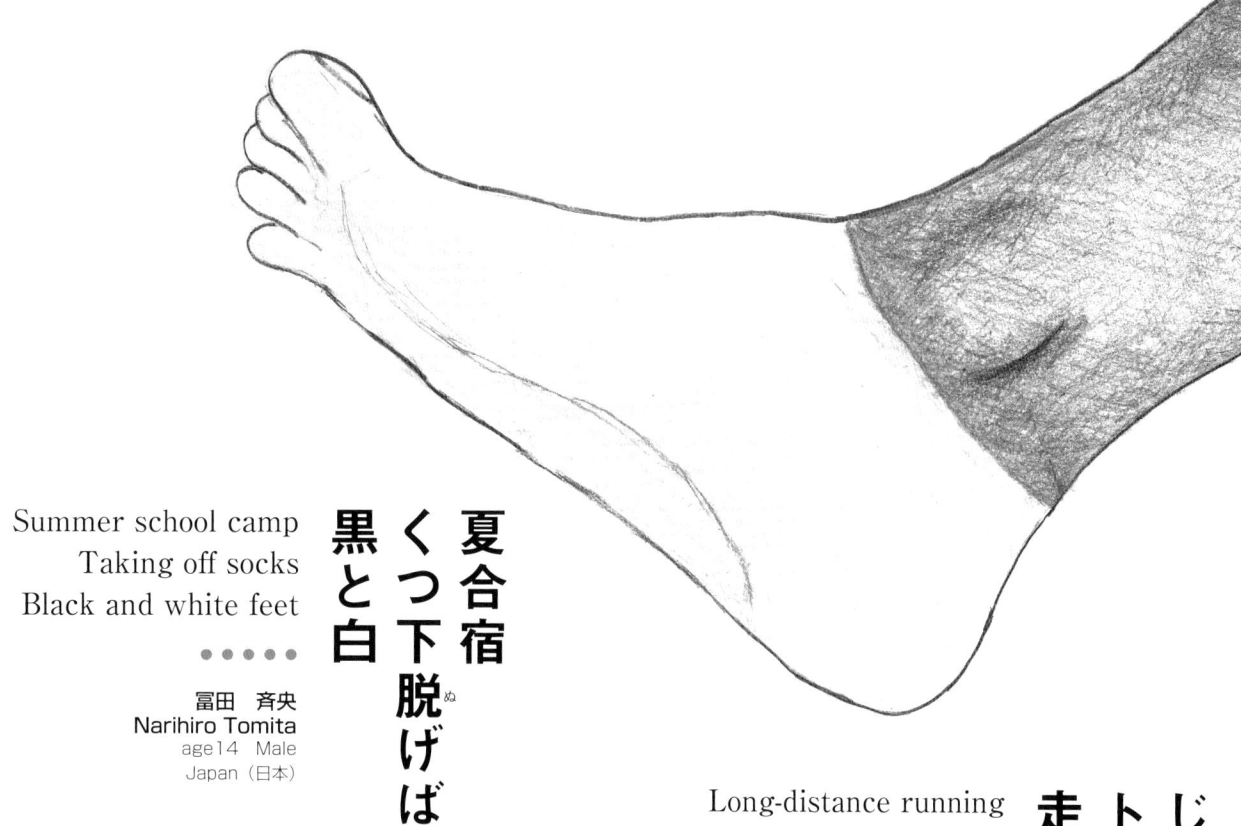

冨田 斉央
Narihiro Tomita
age14 Male
Japan（日本）

Long-distance running
Dragonflies have joined us
Aren't they so swift, though

じきゅう走
トンボもいっしょに
走ってる

・・・・・

小木曽 若菜
Wakana Ogiso
age 9 Female
Japan（日本）

"Get set" and five seconds to go
My heart bursting
Bang

5秒前
心臓ばく発
よーいドン

・・・・・

黒田 千晶
Chiaki Kuroda
age12 Female
Japan（日本）

雨の中
力を合わせて
大イチョウ

A big ginkgo tree
In a heavy rain
The leaves helping each other
･････

平田 冴
Sae Hirata
age12　Female
Japan（日本）

学校はいろんな色のモザイク
みんなで手をつなごう
だれもぬけないように

School is an mosaic with many colors
We take hands
So nobody is outside

La scuola è un mosaico con tanti colori
Teniamoci per mano
Nessuno resti fuori

● ● ● ● ●

All the class
age10　Male/Female　Italy（イタリア）

秋の風
やさしく校内をふきぬける
暑い夏をふきとばして

柔柔的秋風
輕輕吹遍了校園
吹走了炎夏

Soft autumn wind
Gently blowing through the school
Sweeping away the hot summer

柔柔的秋風
輕輕吹遍了校園
吹走了炎夏

● ● ● ● ●

Tsz Fung Tsang
age9　Male
China（中国）

On a swing
I push up high
Up above a cloud

• • • • •

松井　千夏
Chinatsu Matsui
age9　Female
Japan（日本）

ぶらんこを
いっぱいこいで
雲の上

Waiting for children
Who come racing out from class
Deserted playground

• • • • •

Khatun Anisa
age8　Female
England（イギリス）

運動場
教室とびだす
子らを待つ

Morning sun glistened
All children ready to learn
The school built on love

• • • • •

Xuan Hui Victoria Kang
age9　Female
Singapore（シンガポール）

朝日きらきら
愛情いっぱいの学校
どの子もやる気にあふれてる

She's from the 8th class
I'm in love for the first time
School's good because of her

Ona iz 8.a,
prvič sem bil zaljubljen
Šola je dobra

• • • • •

Tin Troha
age14　Male
Slovenia（スロベニア）

あの子は8組
ひとめぼれ
学校っていいね

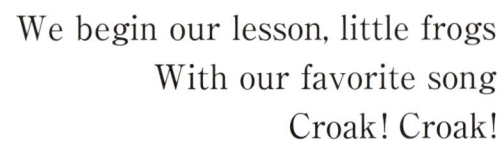

We begin our lesson, little frogs
With our favorite song
Croak! Croak!

Начинаем урок, лягушатки,
С любимой песенки:
Ква-ква!

● ● ● ● ●

Dymchenko Vika
age6　Female
Russia（ロシア）

ちびガエル
お気に入りの歌で授業スタート
くわっ！くわっ！

フクロウの子どもたち
今夜は星の数え方を
教えましょう

Tonight, owlets
I will teach you
To count the stars

Сегодня ночью, совятки,
Я научу вас
Считать звезды.

• • • • •

Shipkova Lera
age8　Female
Russia（ロシア）

リサイクルしよう
環境(かんきょう)を守るため
学校で習ったんだよ

Come and recycle
Help save the environment
I learnt this from school

・・・・・

Wan Ying Lau
age7　Female
Singapore（シンガポール）

校庭に
ハリネズミたちの
足の音

Rustle, crackle, wheeze
The hedgehogs little feet tap
On our schoolground

Raschel, knister, schnauf
die Igelfüßchen tapsen
auf unserm Schulhof

· · · · ·

Sophie Riedel
age10　Female
Germany（ドイツ）

子猫(こねこ)さん、今夜は
月(つき)あかりの屋根(やね)の上で
卒業(そつぎょう)記念(きねん)コンサートだよ

Today, kittens
On the roof, with a clear moon
Graduation concert

Сегодня, кошечки,
На крыше, при ясной луне,
Выпускной концерт.

● ● ● ● ●

Baskakova Nika
age8　Female
Russia（ロシア）

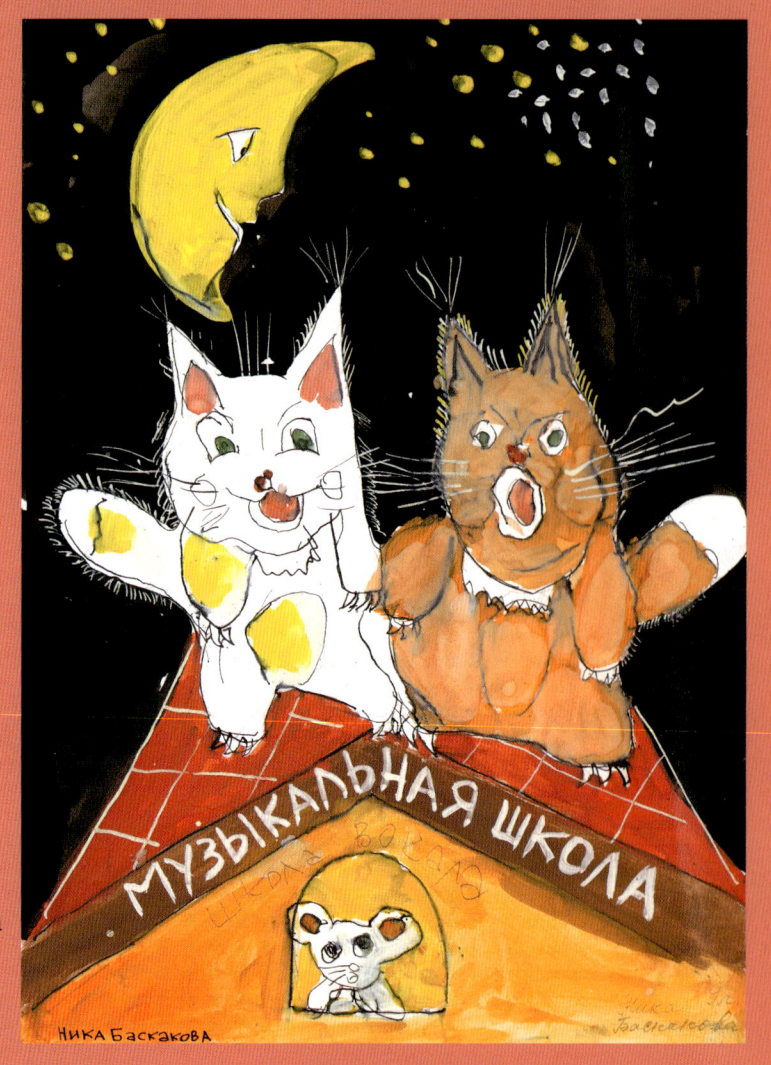

At School we have fun
In the Summer we play games
The teachers are cool

・・・・・

Leah Dodos
age12　Female
Australia（オーストラリア）

夏はゲーム
先生もいけてるし
学校って楽しい

On pencil cases
Autographs hold memories
Friendships forever

・・・・・

Emily-Rose Clemence
age12　Female
New Zealand（ニュージーランド）

ペンケースのサイン
大切な思い出
友情は永遠に

Many children
Learn, listen
And become friends

Tanti bambini imparano,
ascoltano

・・・・・

Francesca Buzzoni
age9　Female
Italy（イタリア）

子どもたち
学んで、きいて
友になる

学校にあつまった
赤・橙(だいだい)・黄・緑・青・藍(あい)・紫(むらさき)
夢の色

Coming together at school
Red・Orange・Yellow・Green・Blue・Indigo・Violet
Color of the dreams

학교에 모인
빨주노초파남보
꿈들의 색깔

● ● ● ● ●

Kim Jiwon
age12　Female
Korea（韓国）

かくれんぼ
木にかくれて数えよう
いち、に、さん……

Playing hide and seek
We are hiding in the tree
Counting one, two, three……

● ● ● ● ●

Ling Hin Chan
age7　Male　China（中国）

Schools of the future
Strive to improve life on earth
Seek progress for man

・・・・・

Mohd Fadil
age11　Male
Singapore（シンガポール）

未来の学校は
地球の暮らしをよくするためにがんばる
人類の進歩を求めて

The school is empty
It is bored
Where are children's shouts?

Пусто в школе.
Школа очень скучает.
Где же детский крик?

・・・・・

Leonov Mihail
age10　Male
Russia（ロシア）

からっぽの学校は
つまらない
子どもたちはどこ？

The bus engine roars
The school trip will soon begin
Adventure awaits

・・・・・

Alex Lye
age 12　Male
New Zealand（ニュージーランド）

うなるバスのエンジン
もうすぐ遠足に出発だ
冒険がまっている

運動場
冬の虫たち
計算の勉強中

In the playground
The insects of the winter
Studying to calculate

Dans la cour de récré
Les insectes de l'hiver
Apprennent à compter

Thomas Deydier
age 14　Female
France（フランス）

木を植える
大きくなって花が咲けば
学校はぼくを思い出すだろう

I plant a tree
Let it grow and blossom
The school will remember me

Сажаю дерево.
Пусть растёт и цветёт.
Школа вспомнит меня.

・・・・・

Styopkin Alexander
age11　Male　Russia（ロシア）

まちがいから
学んで
つぎはきっと成功

My roots of knowledge
Where I learn from my mistakes
So I may succeed

・・・・・

Shana Dilliner
age13　Female
USA（アメリカ）

It passes a bag to everyone
So that we can take
A lot of knowledge out of it

Vsakemu poda
torbo, da iz nje nabere
veliko znanja

・・・・・

Urša Ambrožič
age12　Female
Slovenia（スロベニア）

みんなにカバンがくばられる
たくさんの知識が
得られるように

Wind blows
Outside the window
I can hear laughter

・・・・・

Mio Matsuo
age10　Female
China（中国）

風が吹く
窓の外から
笑い声

Footsteps in the hall
Happy footsteps in the field
Hers, mine, everyone's

・・・・・

Yu-wei, Hannah Teo
age12　Female
Singapore（シンガポール）

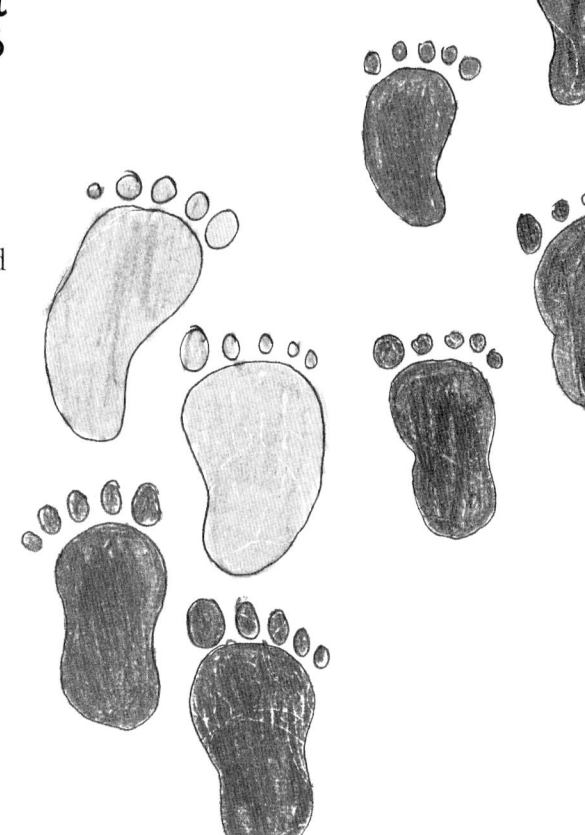

ホールの足音
校庭の楽しそうな足音
彼女の、ぼくの、みんなの足音

おわりに

日航財団では、一九九〇年より二年に一度、「世界こどもハイクコンテスト」を開催しています。二〇〇九〜二〇一〇年にかけて第十一回コンテストが行われ、世界十八の国や地域から今回のテーマである「学校」を詠んだ一万点を超える作品の応募がありました。第十一回大会はコンテスト創設二十年の節目の年でもありますので、この創設の歴史について簡単にご紹介したいと思います。

東京オリンピックが開かれた一九六四年、日本航空は日本文化を海外へ紹介する事業の一つとして俳句をとりあげ、米国のラジオ番組を通じて「ハイクコンテスト」を行ったところ、全米から四万通をこえるハイクが投稿されました。この呼びかけが、日本につながるコンテストの始まりでした。その後、英国、カナダ、豪州で、各国の子どもたちや教師が大変に関心を示し、応募作品も想像以上に素晴らしいものでした。世界最短詩であるハイクに子どもたちや教師が大変に関心を示し、応募作品も想像以上に素晴らしいものでした。これらのコンテストをとおして、俳句というものが海外でも受け入れられることを知り、一九九〇年には日本航空の海外支店網を活用して、世界中の子どもたちを対象とした「第一回世界こどもハイクコンテスト」を実施しました。その後、各国の学期制度の違いから、毎年ではなく、二年に一度コンテストを開催することとし、翌年には優秀作品を『地球歳時記』として出版する形が定着し、今日に至っています。

「世界こどもハイクコンテスト」の作品は、ハイクと絵で構成されています。子どもたちに豊かな感性を育んでほしいとの願いから、ハイクに加え、詠んだときの目の前の光景や記憶にある情景を自らの手で描きとめてもらうことにしています。彼らの作品は俳句という日本の形式を借りており、子どもの作品であるにもかかわらず、そこにお国柄を垣間見ることができます。また、絵に描いてみせることで、自国に居ながらにして異国の豊かな感性に触れるとともに、世界中の多彩な自然に触れることができ、自国に居ながらにして異国を理解することができるのも『地球歳時記』の特徴の一つです。

ハイクをとおして日本や日本文化を理解するだけでなく、世界の子どもたちが感動をわかちあい、相互理解が深まっていくこと。そして遠い異国に住んでいても、同じハイクでつながることができるんだということを『地球歳時記』を通じて実感していただければと考えています。

最後に、このコンテストは、日本のみならず世界各国の学校の先生方をはじめとする教育機関の皆様、選考にご協力いただいた日本学生俳句協会、海外でコンテスト運営にご協力いただいた日本航空、ブロンズ新社など、多くの関係の皆様のご協力のもと実施しております。この場をお借りして、心より御礼を申し上げます。

財団法人 日航財団
常務理事 中川浩昌

＊「ハイク」‥日本語の五七五で詠まれる「俳句」に対し、海外の母国語で詠まれる三行の詩を「ハイク」と表現しています。

Epilogue

Since 1990, the JAL Foundation has hosted the World Children's Haiku Contest every two years. The 11th Contest was held during 2009-2010, with participants from 18 countries and regions of the world submitting over 10,000 haiku composed under the theme of "School". As the 11th Contest fell on its 20-year milestone anniversary, we would like to present a brief history of this activity.

In 1964, when the Olympic Games were held in Tokyo, Japan Airlines took up haiku as a part of its endeavors aimed at introducing traditional Japanese culture overseas, and sponsored a haiku contest in the U.S. through an American radio program. There were over 40,000 entries from people of all ages. We expanded the contests to the United Kingdom, Canada, and Australia, with children as the target. In each country, children as well as teachers showed significant interest in haiku, the world's shortest from of poetry, and the works submitted were of much higher quality than anticipated. Through those contests, we came to believe that haiku could be well received overseas. In 1990, through Japan Airlines' network of overseas offices, we held the first World Children's Haiku Contest for children worldwide. Later, in order to accommodate the differences in the beginning and ending times of each country's school year, the Contest has been held biennially rather than annually, with highly-rated entries being published in book form in the following year.

The works submitted to the World Children's Haiku Contest consist of haiku poems and drawings. In hopes of encouraging children to cultivate and develop their sensibility, we ask them, in addition to composing haiku, to draw pictures of the actual scenes or mental images that they see when they compose haiku. Despite the fact that the works are in a Japanese form of poetry and that the composers are all children, their works do provide glimpses of the characteristics of the poets' home countries. Through the children's pictures, we can be touched by the great sensitivity of children in those tender years, as well as the colorful natural scenery of different parts of the world. This "Haiku by World Children" provides us with an opportunity to enhance our understanding of other countries while staying in our own.

It would be our great pleasure if "Haiku by World Children" helps you to realize that world children can not only understand Japan and its culture through haiku, but share their excitement and deepen mutual understanding, and also that children living in different corners of the world can be linked together through haiku.

Lastly, this Contest is made possible by the generous support provided by various individuals and organizations - teachers and other professionals working at educational institutions in Japan and other countries, the Japan Student Haiku Association who assisted in the selection of haiku, the employees of Japan Airlines who cooperated in managing the contests overseas, and Bronze Publishing Inc., just to name a few. We express our hearty gratitude to all of them for their contributions.

Hiromasa Nakagawa
Managing Director
JAL Foundation

Kaitlin Jakson-Crates   50
Cameron Smith   58
Cameron Flannery   59
Emily-Rose Clemence   73
Alex Lye   75

Philippines フィリピン

Maria Frencheska Nueva   13
Danielle Royon   35
Princess Vhe Bacolod   55
Patrick Sotto   60

Russia ロシア

Rzhevkina Nina   カバー, 35
Scherbakova Dasha   5
Besedina Sasha   9
Zaitseva Natalya   18
Nikitin Fyodor   20
Kuzmin Fedya   31
Samsonov Kostya   32
Mescheryakova Agrippina   36
Muhametzyanova Elina   36
Danilova Ekaterina   40
Baiguzina Yulia   41
Surikov Oleg   43
Golubeva Alisa   49
Groza Lyuba   53

Mohova Ekaterina   55
Konzhets Nikolai   60
Dymchenko Vika   68
Shipkova Lera   69
Baskakova Nika   72
Leonov Mihail   75
Styopkin Alexander   77

Singapore シンガポール

Xuan Hui Victoria Kang   1, 67
Joanne Ng   19
Yi Kai Choo   26
Darren Yeo   27
Wai Yann Lam   45
Nadia Natasha Binte Abdul Rashid   51
Xu Ruo Gillian Chen   51
Victoria Lynn Chin   56
Wan Ying Lau   70
Mohd Fadil   75
Yu-wei, Hannah Teo   79

Slovenia スロベニア

Ferjančič Polona   50
Tin Troha   67
Urša Ambrožič   79

Thailand タイ

Pattamon Pattanaitsaraporn   カバー, 33
Thanakrit Muangsri   11
Sireejitt Srisuwan   14
Mata Jakpeng   15
Kaennita Kambud   25
Komkrid Saekong   28
Dararat Khamjing   29
Patcharaporn Bootrod   31
Phattaraporn Udjai   47
Napat Saeong   48

Turkey トルコ

Selin Mihaloglu   33

USA アメリカ

Rachel Ying   12
Keymon Robinson   17
Gwynette Paez   30
Tyler Caro   42
Kerrick Chinen   53
Puniwaiwai Lua-Medeiros   59
Ethan Siegfried   60
Shana Dilliner   78

INDEX

Australia オーストラリア
Bella Huggins 11
Georgina Sarah 46
Mia Smith 54
Stephanie Wong 60
Leah Dodos 73

China 中国
Yuen Ching Ho 8
Agape Luk 21
Martin Lee 22
Po Nam Anson Lam 39
Wai Ping Patricia Wong 59
Tsz Fung Tsang 66
Ling Hin Chan 74
Mio Matsuo 79

Croatia クロアチア
Anita Bagarić 57
Lucia Pulek 57

England イギリス
Cullum Myles 10
Gill Ramneet 24

France フランス
Duggleby William 44
Lester Michael 53
Woolf Ellen 53
Anderson Ivan 57
Hammond Amy 58
Khatun Anisa 67

France フランス
Linda Benkhelifat 59
Thomas Deydier 76

Germany ドイツ
Caroline Weinz 7
Jakob Schornholz 38
Michell Koczirka 52
Lukas Maidhof 61
Sophie Riedel 71

Italy イタリア
Valeria Fusco 31
Leda Orengo 34
Francesco Maria Picchi 38
Ilaria Paglia 43
Caterina Cestari 57
All the class 65
Francesca Buzzoni 73

Japan 日本
Yousuke Tsuhako 6
Tae Fujii 7
Ryo Kidachi 11
Mizuka Shinagawa 35
Hirotaka Sugawara 62
Chiaki Kuroda 63
Narihiro Tomita 63
Wakana Ogiso 63
Sae Hirata 64
Chinatsu Matsui 67

Korea 韓国
Kim Jiwon 74

Morocco モロッコ
Alessandra Landogna 16
Charles Posez 37

New Zealand ニュージーランド
Miles Dover 23
Harry White 26
Amelia Anderson 36
Morgan Adams 36
Hannah Hyunju Ban 49

地球歳時記
がっこうのうた
Impressions of school

2011年4月25日　初版第1刷発行

編　者　日航財団

装丁者　籾山真之（snug.）
発行者　若月眞知子
発行所　（株）ブロンズ新社
　　　　東京都渋谷区神宮前 6-31-15-3B
　　　　03-3498-3272
　　　　http://www.bronze.co.jp/

印　刷　吉原印刷
製　本　田中製本印刷

©2011　JAL FOUNDATION
ISBN978-4-89309-518-3 C8076

本書に掲載されている、全ての文章及び画像等の無断転用を禁じます。

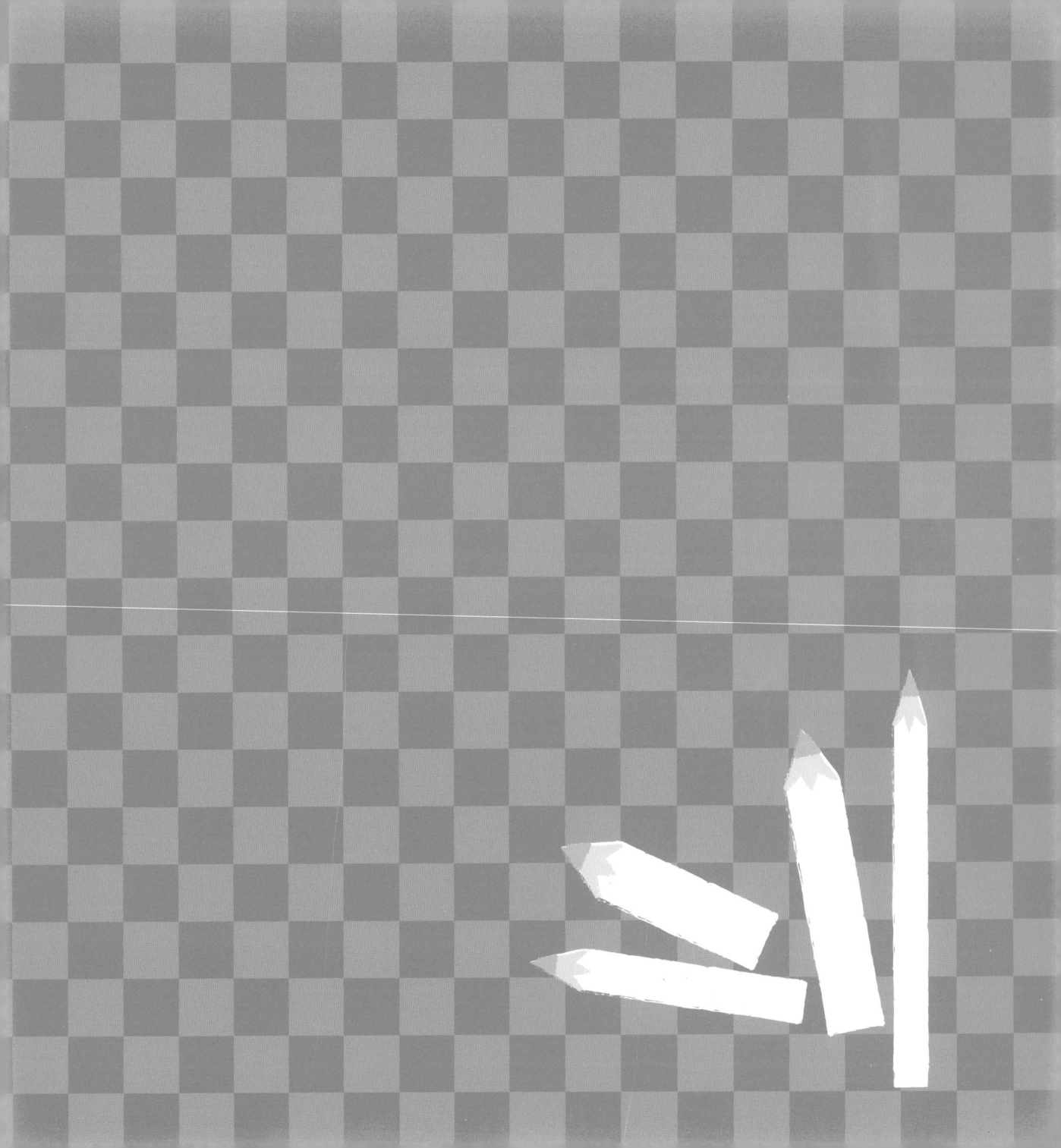